A BANANA BOOK

The Quest of the Golden Dragon

June Counsel

Illustrated by
ROBERT BARTELT

HEINEMANN · LONDON

S. Needs

William Heinemann Ltd
Michelin House
81 Fulham Road, London SW3 6RB
LONDON · MELBOURNE · AUCKLAND

First published 1987
Reprinted 1991
Text © June Counsel 1987
Illustrations © Robert Bartelt 1987

A school pack of BANANA BOOKS 19-24 is
available from Heinemann Educational Books
ISBN 0 435 00103 5

ISBN 434 93042 3
Printed in Italy by Olivotto

Sharp shows where

THREE PIRATES SAT grumbling round
a driftwood fire.

'I'm getting a bit old for this sort of
lark,' growled Swagger the Captain.
'Another fight like that last one and I
won't live to tell the tale.'

'Those Spaniards crept up on us in
the dark,' grumbled First Mate Swash,
'we never heard them come.'

'But we can't give it up,' sighed
Buckle the Bo'sun. 'It's the only trade
we know.'

'Sir, sir,' came a pipy voice behind them. 'Have you heard of the Golden Dragon that warns its owner when danger's coming?'

'Eh up!' cried the pirates. 'Where's this Golden Dragon then?'

'It belongs to some Chinese merchants so we need to go to China,' said Sharp the cabin boy, coming round with the rum. 'I can show you where on the map when we go aboard.'

Swagger leaped to his feet and tossed the last of his rum on to the fire. 'Then China it is!' he cried. 'Ahoy for the Golden Dragon, if so be as Sharp will show us where!'

He clumped down the beach to the dinghy and Buckle rowed them all back to the Magpie, where she rode at anchor in the bay. Sharp got a large map out of the chart locker in the wheelhouse and unrolled it carefully.

'There, sir,' said Sharp, pointing to a black dot on a wriggling blue line. 'In that town on that river. We'll need disguises, of course. I could make them, if you'd let me, sir.'

'I'll let you,' said Swagger.

The Golden Dragon is captured

IN A GARDEN by a yellow river, two Chinese merchants were praising a golden dragon. It was no bigger than a fist and stood on a jade-green table overlooking a lake of waterlilies. The merchants were beating gongs and chanting, swaying backwards and forwards with their eyes closed:

> Great dragon of gold
> Wise dragon of old
> Smeller of strangers
> Warner of dangers.

A red lacquered bridge arched over the lake and tiptoeing over it came four Chinese workmen in loose, blue cotton jackets and trousers, with wide straw hats that shaded their faces. Three were big, one was small, all carried buckets.

'*Hiss*,' went the Golden Dragon when it saw them. 'Hiss, hiss, hiss.' But the merchants were lost in their chanting and gonging and, moreover, their eyes were closed. They fell to their knees, tucking their gongs in their wide silk sleeves and touched the ground with their foreheads. The four Chinese workmen crept closer.

'*Spit, spit,*' went the Golden Dragon desperately. Then indeed the merchants heard it and leaped up, but too late, too late! Two buckets went over their heads, a third scooped up the Golden Dragon, and a fourth hit their bucketted heads such a bonk that they toppled over into the lake and went glugging and spluttering among the waterlilies.

Then the four Chinese workmen went running back over the bridge, leaped down the bank, jumped into a dinghy and rowed back across the river and through a screen of weeping willows beyond which, in an inlet of an island, the Magpie lay hidden.

There they tossed off their straw hats, tore off their drooping false moustaches and rolled about the deck, laughing their heads off.

'Oh, oh, matey, you're ours now,' gasped Swagger, holding the Golden Dragon before his eyes. 'You warn *us* of danger now.'

'Hurray!' chortled Swash, 'we'll be masters of the Seven Seas and top of the Pirate League.'

'Well done, Sharp lad,' cried Buckle, slapping Sharp on the shoulder. 'Sharp by name and sharp by nature, that's you. We've never had a cabin boy like you before.'

'Nor you never have,' smiled Sharp, who was not modest.

The Chinese merchants hauled themselves out of the lake, shook the goldfish out of their sleeves, tidied up the waterlilies and sent their fastest junks and their smartest sailors after the Magpie, but the Golden Dragon kept such a careful watch that they could not catch her. For the Golden Dragon worked for whoever owned it. The crew of the Magpie owned it now, so it hissed and spat for them.

That summer was the best season the Magpie had ever had. The crew took so much treasure, they grew fat and greedy and careless, all except Sharp, who didn't care for drinking and would sooner shin up the rigging than gorge in the cabin.

Swagger makes a mistake

ONE DAY WHEN they were passing an island, a boat put out with an old woman in it, who hailed them. She stood bending and swaying, holding on to the mast, while she called up to them:

'Do you want a cook? I can make a meal a king would beg for.'

In the galley, Sharp heard a furious spitting and thought a pot was boiling over, but looking up saw there was nothing on the stove but an old saucepan simmering quietly. Racing up

9

on deck to the wheelhouse where the
Golden Dragon was kept, Sharp saw it
hissing and spitting for all it was worth,
but the crew had their backs to it, and
were leaning over the side listening to
an old woman.

'Take me on board, gentlemen,'
Sharp heard the old woman say, 'And
I'll cook you dishes you've only
dreamed about, with afters and seconds
and . . .'

'Don't listen to her, Cap'n, sir,' cried

Sharp. 'She's dangerous. Listen to the Golden Dragon. It's hissing like a steam kettle.'

'Oh, take no notice,' shouted Swagger, who was fond of his food. 'Granny here won't harm anyone and, no offence, Sharp lad, but we could do with a change of menu.'

He offered his arm to the old woman who had climbed the rope ladder let down to her, but she waved it aside and leapt nimbly down on to the deck and her boat scudded back to shore by itself.

'There, see,' cried Sharp. 'That's not natural.' But Swagger was leading the old woman down to the galley and Swash and Buckle were following, rubbing their hands and laughing.

That evening the old woman cooked a meal that made the pirates gobble and

gulp like guzzling pigs, it was so rich
and mouth-watering, and afterwards
she brewed some punch that made
them silly and sleepy.

She took a glass of it up to Sharp
for the cabin boy had refused to share
the feast and had gone on deck with
only a couple of ship's biscuits.

'Drink this, dearie,' the old woman
smiled, her leathery skin crinkling into
yellow creases. 'It'll make a man of you.'

There was a sudden hiss behind her.
She started and turned round. When
she saw the Golden Dragon she looked
at it evilly. Sharp raised the glass, and
took a mouthful smiling, but when the
old woman had gone back to the galley,
Sharp walked to the side, spat out the
mouthful and tossed the glass and its
contents into the sea.

'I will not be made a man of,' said
Sharp to the waves.

Below in the galley, the old woman

began to croon to herself as she washed
the dishes and, presently, a little wind
got up and made white caps to the
waves. She raised her voice and the
wind blew stronger and the waves flung
their spray into Sharp's face. She sang
faster and shriller and the wind tore
through the rigging and the waves
tossed the Magpie about like a
shuttlecock. Terrified, Sharp struggled
across the pitching deck and down to
the cabin where the pirates sat, redfaced
and stupid.

'Captain,' bawled Sharp in Swagger's
ear, 'we need to take in sail.'

But Swagger could only belch and
burp, so Sharp went to Swash and
shook him. 'There's a gale blowing, sir,
we're shipping water.' But the First
Mate only stared at his glass and
smiled.

Then Sharp grabbed the Bo'sun by the shoulder and shook him, 'Oh, Mr Buckle, sir, we're going to sink!'

'Easy, lad, easy,' muttered Buckle, but he began to lumber to his feet. Pushing, shoving, tugging, pulling, fighting wind and water, Buckle and Sharp got the other two up on deck and began to rope them to whatever was loose and would float. Then Sharp tied Buckle to a barrel and Buckle roped Sharp to a plank. The last knot had just been tied when a wave like a green hill fell on the Magpie and thrust her under.

What Sharp saw

NEXT MORNING, the sun, struggling
out of a bed of clouds, shone on four
bodies lying limply on the sandy beach
of the island. The bodies were much
banged about and one, the smallest, was
bleeding from a cut on the forehead.
Lengths of frayed rope trailed about
them and scattered around were the
barrels, planks and spare spars that had
saved their lives. The sun rose higher
and its rays began to warm the sodden
heaps. The smallest one, who had an

old pea-jacket on, sat up and put a hand
to its forehead.

'Oh, my goodness,' groaned Sharp,
looking round and beginning to count.
'Cap'n Swagger, and First Mate Swash,
and look there's Mr Buckle. Thank
goodness, we're all saved, but where's
the old woman?'

There was no other sign of life on
the beach, but a deep furrow ran from
the sea, past the pirates and up the
beach where it disappeared over some
high sand dunes. Much puzzled, Sharp
got up and began to follow the furrow.
As the first sand dune loomed up, a
spluttery hissing, punctuated by
sneezes, began.

'Oh, dragon, are you still there?'
whispered Sharp joyfully, for Sharp had
remembered to snatch up the Golden
Dragon and thrust it deep into the

pocket of the old pea-jacket before
leaving the wheelhouse to warn the
crew, and now here it was, warning of
danger.

'All right, dragon, I'll take care.'

Dropping down, Sharp began to crawl
up the sand dune on hands and knees,
but the hissing continued so the cabin
boy fell flat to the sand and wriggled up
the last slope like a snake till it was just

possible to peer over the topmost ridge.

An indrawn hiss that was Sharp, not the dragon, and 'Oh, dragon,' breathed Sharp, taking in the view with goggling eyes, 'we're done for now!'

A living meal

A SCALY SEA WITCH was coiled in
the hollow talking to her seven slithery
children.

'Such treats I've got for you! Three
fat sailors for the big ones and one boy
sailor for you, my littlest!'

The slithery children began to squeal
and squirm.

'Oh, Mother, you are clever! Did they
guess you were a sea witch in disguise?'

'No, indeed, as if your mother would
be as stupid as that.'

'Mother, do they know about the guessing game?' inquired the smallest slithery child anxiously, 'do they know that if one of them asks a question we can't answer, we turn to stone?'

'Of course not,' laughed the sea witch, 'as if I'd tell them that! Now come and get your dinner.'

Sharp wriggled backwards down the dune as fast as an eel, if an eel can wriggle backwards, and raced back to the pirates to warn them, but saw by their horrified faces that the scaly sea witch and the seven slithery children had topped the rise already and were coiling down the beach towards them.

Swagger turned white and tried to run, but the sea witch was on him, twining her coils round him like living rope, her eyes and teeth glinting and grinning in her wicked face.

'Come on, children, I'll hold him for you while you begin.'

'He'll be tough,' cried Sharp, dancing round her, 'how old do you think he is?'

'Younger than I am,' grinned the sea witch and watched while the first two slithery children slithered up to take their first bite.

'Leggo,' shouted Swash, hanging on
to a rock, but two other slithery
children wrapped their coils round his
arms and began hauling him forward.

'You won't pull him over,' jeered
Sharp, throwing sand at them. 'How
much do you think he weighs?'

'Less than that rock,' answered the
slithery children and began to nibble.

Buckle fell to his knees. 'Don't eat me, please,' he begged. 'I'm a family man.'

'Leave him be,' commanded Sharp, beating at them with a long strand of seaweed as the last two, but one, slithery children laid hold of Buckle.

'How many children do you think he's got?'

'More than Mother,' answered the slithery children, with their mouths full.

Sharp felt a cold touch on the leg. The youngest slithery child had writhed up with open mouth.

'Hey, hey,' cried Sharp, skipping back, 'what do you think I am?'

'A skinny little *boy* and my di—'

began the youngest slithery child and turned to stone. In mid-munch the other six slithery children and their mother, the sea-witch, turned to stone and all their coils stopped moving.

'Phew!' gasped Sharp, wriggling out of the stone coils, 'that was a near thing.'

Running to the others, the cabin boy rolled the stone monsters off them. The pirates were bleeding freely. Tearing strips from Buckle's shirt, which was pretty torn already, Sharp bathed their wounds with sea water, then bound them tightly, but still the pirates bled and, presently, they lay still and closed their eyes.

'It's all up with us, lad,' whispered Swagger, 'we're a-drifting to Davy Jones's locker. You were right lad, that old Granny wasn't what she seemed.'

'Don't die, oh, don't die,' cried
Sharp, pulling the Golden Dragon out
and looking at it beseechingly. 'Oh,
Golden Dragon, help us, do, please help
us.'

The end of the pirates

THE GOLDEN DRAGON gave a sad
hiss and, looking round, Sharp saw a
Chinese junk lying off shore. It was the
junk that had chased them the longest
and hardest all summer. A boat put out
from it and came rowing to the shore
with the two Chinese merchants sitting
in the bows. Sharp ran towards it,
holding out the Golden Dragon, ready
to give it to the first hand that reached
for it.

The boat grounded. The Chinese

sailors leaped ashore and helped the merchants to land.

Sharp saw that each sailor carried a sword.

'We have come to take back our dragon and cut off your heads,' called the merchants.

'Don't kill my friends, they're dying,' sobbed Sharp. 'Here's your Golden Dragon. Kill me if you want, it was my plan, but save Captain Swagger and First Mate Swash and Bo'sun Buckle, please, *please*.'

The merchants stared at Sharp,
puzzled, then one of them took the
Golden Dragon and put it in his wide
silk sleeve. Then he nodded to the
sailors and they all followed Sharp to
where the three pirates lay still with
the sand turning red beneath them.

The merchants bent over the curious
stone shapes lying near the pirates

while Sharp jerked out the story in
sniffs and sobs.

'A strange story,' observed one of the
merchants and picked up the smallest
slithery child, now a curving grey rock.
He said something to the sailors who
ran swiftly back to the boat and came
back with six oars, two cloaks and a
sail. Out of these they made three

stretchers. They lifted the pirates on to the stretchers and carried them back to the boat and rowed them out to the junk.

There the Chinese merchants' own doctor, with Sharp's help, cut away the pirates' bloodstained clothes and dressed their wounds. It took a long time and Sharp felt wobbly and faint, but managed to hold the basin and hand the scissors and pass the bandages until the last pirate was clean and comfortable. Then the cabin began to spin round, the doctor's voice went a long way away and Sharp went falling, falling, into a bottomless pit.

The cabin boy came to, lying on a low carved bed beneath a red paper lantern that swung from the deckhead above. The merchants and the doctor were looking down at the bed. On a

stool by it, within reach of Sharp's
hand, was a pile of clothes, neatly
folded. Sharp recognised them; the old
pea-jacket was at the bottom.

'Ah, you see that we know all about
you,' nodded one of the merchants. 'So,
tell us why you went to sea.'

'I wanted adventure,' replied Sharp, looking up at them. 'I was brought up in an orphanage. They made me work like a servant. It was lonely and cold, and so *dull*. So I disguised myself and ran away to sea.'

'Yes,' nodded the merchants, 'you are good at disguises. You were the one who stole our Golden Dragon, weren't you?'

Sharp nodded and began to grin, seeing again the bright lake with the two bucketted heads bobbing about among the waterlilies. A giggle escaped. Then, meeting the merchants' serious eyes, Sharp stopped giggling and, presently, began to feel ashamed and blushed.

'I'm sorry,' said Sharp. 'It was just a lark. We didn't mean to hurt you. Don't kill my friends. I made all the plans. They'd never have worked out the bucket business; they're really only good at fighting and sailing.'

'We have our Golden Dragon back,' said the merchants. 'We know where the Magpie sank, so we can salvage the treasure and return it to its rightful owners. Your friends are too badly hurt to go pirating again. What would they like to do, do you know?'

'Keep a pub,' said Sharp promptly, 'they've often talked about doing that.'

'Then we will not kill them. We will not even tell anyone that they were once pirates. As for you,' said the merchants, looking down at Sharp sternly, 'no more disguises! Be yourself, and be honest. We will send some clothes to you.'

Buckle, opening his eyes from an opium-induced sleep, saw a Chinese vision standing in front of him.

'I always said you was a most uncommon cabin boy, Sharp,' he murmured, 'that yellow silk robe with them butterflies embroidered on it does go pertickler well with that yellow hair of yourn.' Then he closed his eyes and drifted off again into healing sleep.

A toast to Sharp

MANY MONTHS LATER, three ex-
pirates sat round a fire of apple logs.
Outside the autumn dusk grew chill
and the inn sign hung motionless.

'There'll be a frost tonight,' remarked
Swagger. 'I feel it in my wooden leg.'
This was a joke of his. He often said he
felt things in his wooden leg. 'Close the
shutters, Mr Mate.'

'Aye, aye, sir,' said Swash, and began
to pull out the wooden shutters from
where they were folded back by the

side of each window. He had a steel
hook where his right hand had been,
and was astonishingly deft with it.
'Sharp painted that sign a treat,' he
growled, looking up through the last
window. 'That bird seems to cock its
eye right at you.'

The sign was a magpie with its head
on one side.

39

'Sharp will be along with the candles,' said Swagger. 'Pour us a measure each, Bo'sun. We'll drink to The Magpie, the best kept pub for sailors on all the coasts of England.'

Buckle began to pour. In spite of the patch over one eye, he was still a good pourer. He had a measuring eye and never spilled a drop.

A yellow glow of candlelight joined the
firelight as a sharp-featured girl came
into the room carrying a tray of lighted
candles. She set the candles about the
room and then came to the table.

'We've had a wonderful season, thanks
to you, so we're going to drink a toast to
The Magpie,' said Swagger.

'Oh, I'll drink to that,' smiled Sharp, taking a glass. The candlelight shone on her yellow hair and showed up the scar on her forehead. 'To the best crew there ever was,' she said.

The three men raised their glasses. 'To Captain Sharp,' they cried. 'Where would we be without her?'